TE

With love to my mother . . .
funny, hardworking, selfless,
and slightly crazy—M.C.S.

For Alison, without you
none of this would be possible.—S.B.

OXFORD
UNIVERSITY PRESS

Great Clarendon Street, Oxford OX2 6DP
Oxford University Press is a department of the University of Oxford.
It furthers the University's objective of excellence in research, scholarship,
and education by publishing worldwide. Oxford is a registered trade mark
of Oxford University Press in the UK and in certain other countries

Text copyright © Oxford University Press 2019
Illustrations copyright © Steve Brown 2019
Author photo © Mary Stevens

The moral rights of the author have been asserted

Database right Oxford University Press (maker)

First published 2019

British Library Cataloguing in Publication Data

Data available

WARRIOR MONKEYS AND THE DEADLY TRAP

M.C. STEVENS

ILLUSTRATED BY
STEVE BROWN

OXFORD
UNIVERSITY PRESS

MEET THE CHARACTERS

SUKI

BEKKO

FARA

CHAN

SENSEI
RIKA

PROLOGUE

'Yunnan! YUNNAN! Where is that dratted servant? Yunnan! My tea is cold!' Jirugi, an angry mandrill, stamped on the thin floor of his tree house, causing the branches to creak beneath him. 'Get yourself up here right now before I trim your tail! Yu—oh, there you are! How dare you enter without bowing!'

A snub-nosed monkey had hurtled into the room. He backed up rapidly and knelt at the edge of the room. 'Lord Jirugi. So sorry, sir. Your tea. So sorry, sir. You have a visitor. So sorry, sir.'

Jirugi's angry face brightened at the news of a visitor. 'Ah! Finally he has arrived! Show him in straight away. And get me more tea immediately.'

Yunnan remained kneeling, looking confused. He tried to speak but didn't dare.

'What are you waiting for, fool?' Jirugi snarled at him.

'Sir . . . you want me to show him in. And get the tea? Which do you want me to do first? So sorry, sir. I want to serve you well.' Yunnan was not brave enough to look up, which was probably just

as well as his master answered him by throwing the teacup at him. It bounced off his head, smashing on the floor.

'What am I reduced to, with only this ignorant servant to help me? Send in our guest. Then get us both tea. And apologize to him for this rude delay. You're insulting us both with your stupidity.'

Yunnan was nearly in tears at his master's cruel words. He bowed and started backing out of the room, still on his knees.

Jirugi was not finished yet, however. 'Where are you going? Can't you see this mess? How can you bring a visitor up here when there is a broken cup on the floor? Clear it up now!'

'Yes, sir. So sorry, Lord Jirugi.' Poor
Yunnan was having a bad day. For Jirugi,
however, it was a good day. He couldn't
wait to explain his plan to the visitor.
A new plan to get his revenge on the
Warrior Monkeys of Senshi Island!

The visitor listened carefully but
seemed unsure. Jirugi brushed aside
any concerns. 'They'll welcome you in.
Trusting imbeciles.'

'But, Jirugi, sir,' stammered his
companion. 'How can you be sure?'

'I know these blockheads.' Jirugi spoke
with contemptuous certainty. 'Just tell
them you want to learn their ways; they

love to try and teach people to be fair, to be nice, to be . . . ugh . . . so weak! Gain their confidence. Find me the Kokoro medal. Then I will have my revenge. I will be unstoppable!'

CHAPTER ONE

'Is it dangerous, Sensei? Is it secret?
Will we be back in time for dinner?
Will Kuma find us if we get lost?' Suki's
excited questions bounced out quickly as
she hopped up and down next to Sensei
Rika: Guardian of Senshi.

Her teacher sighed and waited until the
little monkey had to pause for breath.
'Our guard bears cannot access the vault,
Suki, I've told you that before. You can

tell Kuma about it later. And it's not going to be dangerous if you both do exactly as I say.'

The second monkey was Suki's best friend, Bekko. His excitement stayed inside his buzzing brain. Was it excitement, or was it anxiety? He didn't really know. He carried a flat, smooth pebble in his pocket; it felt warm and soothing as his thoughts scudded about. He did know the answers to some of Suki's questions though, because he knew a lot about the history of Senshi Castle and the Warrior Monkeys. 'Kuma cannot come down to the vault because it's not safe for a bear, Suki,' he explained. 'The guard bears are too big and slow for

the vault's protections.' In his head, he wondered if he, too, might be too slow to be safe. But he trusted Sensei Rika, and he was also very keen to see the treasures being kept underneath the castle.

Together they followed Sensei Rika across the courtyard, behind the well, and into a narrow, overgrown passageway between the kitchen garden and the water garden.

She checked that they were alone and then pointed at the broad stone wall. 'Suki, can you see that slightly bigger stone near the top of the wall?'

Suki jumped up to the top of the wall and touched the stone indicated by Rika. 'This one, Sensei?' She pushed it, tried to wobble it, twist it . . . nothing happened.

Rika laughed at her efforts. 'Yes, that one. Now, Bekko, can you see a similar stone near the bottom of the wall?'

Bekko crawled along the base of the wall and found a near-identical stone. He waited for instructions instead of testing it straight away; his nature was to be respectful and obedient, unlike his adventurous friend.

'OK. You both have to press the stones at the same time.' Rika liked how they immediately connected with each other to do the job.

'Ready, Suki?' Bekko called.

'Yes!' came the enthusiastic response. 'Countdown . . . 3, 2, 1 . . . now!' With

what seemed like only a tiny amount
of pressure, a whole section of the wall
swung away heavily. They could see a
narrow stairway inside the wall. It led
steeply downwards: a few steps visible
but the rest lost in solid darkness.

'Right,' said Rika, with satisfaction.
'Down we go. Take a torch with you.'
They each took a bamboo torch from a
stack in the hollow part of the wall, and
Rika lit them with her fire stone and

striker. She pulled the door closed behind them and led the way down the worn wooden steps. Suki was wide-eyed and brimming with energy as she followed Rika down into the deep embrace of the dark. She could tell the stairway was widening as they went down because the dancing shadows on the walls were getting further and further away until they couldn't be seen at all.

'Now, this is important,' Rika said. 'We're nearly at the first defence. I'm going to leave you briefly so I can light the lamp. You will be in mortal danger if you do not stay exactly where you are.' Her voice was absolutely matter-of-fact; no drama. They were both aware that they needed to cross some lethal defences to reach the vault. This was no time for exploring on their own!

'I'm a bit nervous,' Bekko whispered to Suki as Rika walked away, soon becoming just a moving torch in the absolute blackness. He could tell Suki was not scared at all; she was simply simmering with excitement. She took his arm and gave it an encouraging squeeze.

'We'll be fine. And it's so thrilling! What an adventure! I can't believe we're under the castle!' she whispered back. He felt comforted. It was so much easier to be brave when they were side by side. They both gasped as bright flames burst out of a huge jade lamp on the opposite

side of what appeared to be a huge cavern.

A big 'Wow!' burst from Bekko's mouth, as he tried to absorb what he was seeing. It was beyond his imagination: a cave, but the biggest cave in the world. It was impossible to tell how big, because they could not see the furthest wall despite the brilliance of the magnificent lamp.

From their position on the last few steps, they could now at least see the floor. This was very reassuring after the disorientating darkness. It was flat, sandy, and completely empty. Suki started to move towards Rika as they could see her returning.

'Wait!' Bekko urged her, grabbing her

belt to stop her going forwards.

'There's nothing there!' she said, shaking him off. She knew he was cautious, but it could be annoying when he seemed to be obedient for no reason. She jumped down to the last step and on to the sand.

'SUKI!' bellowed Sensei Rika. 'FREEZE!' Years of training meant that this training command (meaning potential danger) produced an instant reaction. Immediately Suki became a statue, only her nose twitching as she wondered where the threat was in this vast, empty space. Bekko watched with fear and curiosity as Rika moved towards Suki, carefully keeping to the edge of the cavern . . . even though the ground looked identical and flat everywhere. He was relieved when Sensei Rika stood next to Suki.

'Come and join us, Bekko,' she invited, pointing to a spot next to Suki. 'Stand exactly there; no further forwards.' He approached with little steps and stood exactly where she indicated. Looking at the ground, he had begun to figure out how the first defence worked.

'Sensei? Is it . . . quicksand?' he asked, both impressed and terrified.

'Indeed it is. Look!' Sensei Rika took a stone from her pocket and threw it to the ground in front of them. It took no time at all to disappear from view.

Suki was delighted. 'That is the coolest thing I have EVER seen!' she grinned. 'It went so fast! That is AWESOME!'

'It would be a lot less awesome if it were you disappearing forever!' Bekko retorted, a bit annoyed that she wasn't more shocked at how close she had come to stepping into the trap.

'Very true!' Sensei Rika said, with severity. 'Stick to your promise, Suki. We're not playing down here. The ancient guardians were determined that no one could reach the vault without knowing the secrets. So that is the first secret. This is quicksand.'

'How do we cross it?' Bekko asked, looking around. Maybe they could climb along the ceiling. Were there ropes?

'The ancient guardians created a safe path.' Rika drew a diagram in the sand with the end of her staff: one smooth line that ran horizontally then swept back like a figure 7. Then a second, shorter line cutting from the middle of the first.

ス

'The calligraphy strokes must be walked in the right order. That's why no one can come down here alone. This shorter line must be walked after the long line is finished.'

Bekko studied the diagram keenly. 'Is that part of the old symbol for "entrance", Sensei?'

'Correct,' she said. 'You can see why it needs more than one person?'

'Er, not really,' began Suki, whose own writing was not great at the best of times and rarely followed any kind of rules.

This time it was Bekko's turn to be reassuring. 'Don't worry, Suki,' he said. 'I know how the characters of the ancient guardians work. I learned them for fun last year.'

He never stopped surprising her with the number of facts he could learn when he had a special interest in something. In fact, now she thought about it, she seemed to recall a lot of charcoal lines on his walls and a heap of extra library books, although that was never unusual with Bekko.

'If this were being written, then the brushstrokes would be in a strict order. So we start together. Then we wait here while you finish the long path, Sensei?' He knelt by the diagram and marked the spot where the short stroke began.

'Well done, Bekko. Absolutely right.' She patted him on the shoulder with approval as he leapt back up. 'I will walk to the end of the long stroke. Then you two walk alone. When you finish the short line, the entrance will open automatically.'

Suki was looking dubious. 'How wide is the safe path?' she asked. 'Is there a way we can check in case we are near the quicksand? Does it look different? How can we tell if it's OK?'

'I don't know exactly how wide it is,' Rika replied seriously. 'It seems to be wider in some places than in others. I use my stick to test the ground in front of me when I'm not sure. There's no visible difference in the sand.'

Suki nodded firmly. 'OK, Sensei. Got it.' She was ashamed of herself for nearly jumping into the quicksand and was determined to focus on doing everything perfectly with no fuss.

'Let's do this!' Suki and Bekko bumped fists as they set off with Sensei Rika. The jade lantern cast dancing rays of light into the vastness of the giant space. It silhouetted the two little monkeys as they followed their teacher, as ever trusting her to take them safely through any peril. Straight to the corner . . . sharp turn together . . . then Suki and Bekko stood firmly at the junction while Sensei Rika completed the path and lit the lamp at the far end of the cavern. That was their signal to go.

As the lantern burst into life, Bekko took command. 'Stay close,' he said to Suki, stepping out on to the sand. Cautiously, they made their way along: checking the path, stepping, checking the position of the lantern. Path. Step. Lantern. Path. Step. Lantern.

At one point, Bekko misjudged the width of the path and stepped one

foot into the squishy quicksand. In his
scramble to pull it out, he dropped his
torch, and it vanished with a gurgle.

'I've got you! Don't panic!' Suki held
his belt while he pulled his foot out.

'Phew, thanks, Suki! I thought I was
going to fall in completely. It kind of
sucks you down!' Bekko was slightly
shaken but relieved.

'Just as well we're doing this together,' she replied. 'I would have gone under already if it wasn't for you. Guess the ancients were fans of teamwork, just like Sensei Rika.'

Sensei Rika could now be seen edging along the safe ledge by the wall towards the dark shape of another unlit lamp in the corner. As they converged, they could hear a stony rumble.

'Ooooh, Bekko! Look! That shadow! The wall is moving!' Suki's voice was full of wonder. How could such a thing be built? Her respect for the ancient guardians had never been anything like Bekko's hero worship, but she could see this was no simple mechanism. So clever!

'First defence passed. Looks like you'll be needing a new torch, Bekko.' Sensei Rika delved into her backpack to take out another bamboo torch, lit it, and handed it to him. Then she added oil to the bowl of the third jade lamp and ignited it. Brightness erupted into the cavern; the leaping flames brought an enticing sight of the passageway ahead. It looked clear and safe. But Suki was not to be fooled this time. What did the ancients have in store for them down there? She waited for Rika to lead the way.

CHAPTER TWO

Bekko realized he was breathing more easily now they had passed through the quicksand, although the air was musty and unpleasant. The ground was strangely smooth, descending rapidly downwards in a curve. Rika stopped with her torch and pointed above them where there was a huge round hole in the ceiling. They would never have noticed it up there in the dark. What was up there?

'Right,' she said. 'Time for the next trap. There are a couple of ways around this one, but this is the easiest. Wait there. Watch.'

She walked on down the path, counting aloud as she went. '. . . 7, 8, 9 . . . 10. That's enough.' She placed a used torch on the ground quickly before retreating back up the passageway, pulling them both with her into an alcove they hadn't noticed before. For a few more seconds, nothing happened.

Now Bekko realized he was not breathing easily any more. In fact, he was not breathing at all. All his instincts screamed 'DANGER', but he did not know where or what the danger was.

'Um, Bekko? Can you hear something
rumbling?' Suki whispered. There was
definitely a noise from far off. Getting
louder all the time. Louder. Closer. It
sounded like a giant boulder. Like a giant
boulder . . . rolling? Like a giant boulder
rolling very fast down a rocky tube
above them, tumbling into the tunnel in
front of them, and disappearing down

the curved tunnel. They could just see
the remains of the torch utterly smashed
on the ground. Suki shuddered and
wondered if anyone had ever been caught
by this trap. A very quick and flat death
would surely be the result!

'OK, it's safe now! Let's go on.
The vault is just down here.' Sensei
Rika remained utterly composed and
deliberate in her actions as she led them
on, down into the mysterious depths
below Senshi Castle.

Standing in front of another huge jade
lamp, they could see a wall with intricate
patterns and symbols on it. 'The entrance
is another sliding mechanism,' Rika told

them, lighting the lamp. 'Try and figure it out.'

Bekko was already trying to decipher the characters. '"What you look" . . . no, must be "seek . . . is in your . . . nose"? What?'

Suki giggled. 'It's up your nose, Bekko!'

He grinned. 'Yeah, maybe that isn't the right translation. See that symbol there? I think it means both nose and light. It seems to say "the darkest dark is under the lamp".'

'Not bad, Bekko,' Sensei Rika smiled. 'That was a saying of the ancients. It usually means that what you are looking for is sometimes right under your nose. Here it's a simple clue. The switch is under the lamp. Have a look.'

Bekko and Suki both dived under the lamp, prodding and pushing until they found a part that could be moved. With a little pressure, it clicked sideways, and the wall rumbled. The vault was open.

'I can't believe we're really here!' Bekko marvelled. 'Every magical item captured by the Warrior Monkeys. Here in this vault! Right in front of us!'

'Don't forget the final defence is still ahead,' Sensei Rika warned them. 'This one is an abyss. It surrounds the whole vault. No one knows how deep it is, and no one has ever returned if they fall. Stick right by me while I show you where to jump.'

They didn't need to be told again. 'The

ancients had some pretty nasty ideas about how to stop people taking this stuff, didn't they?' Suki commented as she followed Sensei Rika.

'Bad people would take some awful risks to get hold of these objects. And they would do some awful things with them too. So we have to keep them safe. It's our duty.' Rika was clearly not prepared to feel sorry for anyone who suffered the defences of the vault. She lit another lamp. 'Ready to see the most dangerous things in the world?'

'Yes! Show us!' they squealed, big eyes reflecting the lamplight.

The cave was large, and wide. Like the castle's moat, a wide crevasse divided the entrance from the cave's floor up ahead. Bekko was intrigued as well as scared. 'Surely it can't go down forever! Has no one ever tested it?'

Suki could see science in his eyes as he began to think about how one could possibly figure out the depth of the abyss. She was willing to regard it as mortally dangerous and treat it as such! 'Bekko! Focus!' she hissed, grabbing his arm and pulling him after Sensei Rika, who was counting steps along the edge.

'Right,' she said. 'See here where it looks a bit wider? This is where we jump.'

'But Sensei, we can't even see the other side!' Suki squeaked, squinting across the abyss to try and spot a landing place.

'I know. That's the trick. There's a ledge just down there, but you can't see it. You just have to know where it is. Follow me.' With casual grace, Sensei Rika jumped into the dark. They heard her land safely, then she came back into view, climbing up on the opposite side.

'Yikes,' Bekko muttered. 'I don't like this!'

'Go on,' Suki urged him. 'We'll be OK.' She felt a lot more nervous than she sounded; trying not to look down, trying not to think about falling forever, trying to trust that it was easier than it looked.

With a gulp, Bekko took a huge leap. Suki didn't dare to wait any longer, immediately jumping after him. Instead of falling into the darkness, she fell on top of Bekko.

'Ouch!'

'Sorry!'

'Come on up here!' Sensei Rika showed them where to climb. At last they could really look at the vault.

They could see that the floor rose steeply upwards with many layers. On each layer, on a wide stony shelf, there were objects laid out and labelled. Steep steps rose to the top, where a statue of an old monkey looked over the objects, staff in hand.

Bekko pointed at the statue. 'Sensei! Does he have the Kokoro medal?'

'Hang on a minute,' Suki interrupted. 'The Kokoro medal? That's not a real thing! It's just a fairy tale.'

'Oh no, Suki. It is very real,' Rika replied. 'And very important. We don't know much about its powers, but we do believe it protects us. I'll show it to you presently, but let's do the job we came for first. The staff, please.'

'I had nearly forgotten about it!' From her backpack, Suki pulled the broken pieces of a magical staff. 'Bekko, have you got the label?'

'Yes!' He delved into his bag to get the explanation of the staff and its powers that he had prepared. Rika showed them where to put their contribution. It felt good to take a moment and reflect on how they had broken the staff and its spell. Not only had they saved the islands from the attack of the evil Jirugi, but their bravery had also earned them promotion to cadet status and the new red belts they wore so proudly.

Suki's active mind didn't pause for long though. Her eyes began to skate along the shelf and nearly popped out of her head as she read some labels attached to nearby items.

Jumping boots. Confiscated from Jindo banana farm by Guardian Tania of Lanka.

Feathers of flight. Donated by traders who survived air attack off the coast of Gimandesh.

Vision mask. Retrieved from prisoners after a failed attempt to break into this vault.

'Ah! This stuff is so cool! Imagine the fun we could have with it!' Suki burst out.

'Imagine how much chaos you would cause!' chuckled Sensei Rika. 'It's just as well we keep it safe. Enemies wouldn't hesitate to kill for these powers. Friends become enemies when magical powers belong to some but not all. You know this.'

In her heart, Suki knew that this was true. The Warrior Monkeys had used objects of power in the distant past, but their history had been troubled by thefts and rebellions. Hundreds of years ago, the guardians had decided to focus on effort and training, shunning individual use of magical items. And, since then, peace and safety ruled the Shanti Islands. Young monkeys learned to be proud of this heritage; they treasured strength of character over fake skills.

'I know, Sensei,' she replied seriously. 'Magic can corrupt people, even good people. But look at this! A bottle that makes you sing well if you drink from it. You can't blame me for wishing Bekko had one of these!'

'Rude!' laughed Bekko, giving her a shove.

'Watch it!' Sensei said. 'This is the last

place you'd want to lose your balance.
I'm not following you into the abyss!
Let's go and visit the statue. His name is
Yotogi. I wonder if he's pleased with you
both?'

They made their way together up to the
top of the wall of treasures where Yotogi
looked down over the vault. Around his
neck hung the Kokoro medal.

Even in a vault full of magical things, this medal was something special. For a while, Suki and Bekko just looked at it in awe. First they were drawn to the ruby, which really did glow, just as they had been told. Then the setting of the stone, in an intricate golden weaving of hands, caught their imagination.

'The heart of the warrior: a gift of protection!' Bekko recited, remembering his storybooks. 'This symbolizes the power of working together?' he asked, examining the hands overlapping around the ruby.

'We believe so,' Sensei nodded. 'The heart of the warrior is strong: that is the ruby. But the true power of the Warrior

Monkeys is our care for each other: that is why it is set into linked hands. If you look closely, you can even see some are bigger and some are smaller. We believe this is about respecting everyone: big, small, weak, strong. Everyone has their place here.'

'May we touch it?' Suki asked, tentatively. She wasn't sure if something so precious could be handled by a scruffy cadet like herself.

'Go ahead. I trust you to be careful! It is your medal as much as it is mine. We are the warriors it protects.' Sensei let them lift and rotate the medallion, marvelling at its golden beauty. They could feel the fizzing energy of the medal just as she had felt it herself when her own sensei, Master Chan, had brought her here so many years ago.

'Many warriors know about the myth of the medal, but not many know that it is real, and how to find it.' She placed her hands on their shoulders. 'You two have proved your loyalty, and you must vow to protect the medal and stop it falling into enemy hands. Do you make this promise?'

'Sensei, I promise to protect the medal with my life,' Bekko swore, instinctively placing his hand on his heart as he held the medal.

And Suki, watching her friend with his simple loyalty and honesty, found a tear in her eye. Was she worthy of this responsibility? 'Sensei,' she said. 'I vow to protect this medal and the Warrior Monkeys of Senshi with everything I can do, and I will train to be a better warrior so I can protect it even better!'

'That's a good promise, Suki. I make one like it myself every day. We should never stop trying to be better. Now! Who's hungry? Nothing like deadly traps to make you want some dinner!' Sensei led the way out of the vault, leaving the flickering flames of the jade lantern to burn out. Soon the red glow of the ruby medal was the only light remaining in the secret Senshi underground world.

CHAPTER THREE

Suki and Bekko lost no time in going to tell Kuma all about their adventurous morning. The kindly guard bear lived in the gatehouse and enjoyed the visits of his favourite monkey students. He gave them some carrot cake and listened with interest as they chattered excitedly about the vault. He was always keen for them to impress their teachers. 'Sensei Rika must really trust you to show you all that!' he

remarked. 'You're not white belts any more. Red belt comes with privileges and responsibilities.'

'Like our new weapons!' Suki agreed, leaping off her chair and swooshing her stick around.

'Ahem. Yes.' Kuma winced as she narrowly missed whacking his favourite teapot. He moved it quickly, then his jug . . . and some of his carvings. 'It's stick class tomorrow, isn't it?'

'Yes,' confirmed Suki with more dramatic stick swishes. 'I wish it was more fun though! I thought it would be really cool, but Master Tak is sooooo strict and makes us do everything a billion times.' Master Tak was a weapons expert who had recently joined the Senshi community. He drilled the cadets relentlessly. Suki impersonated his voice, pretending to be really boring. *'Strike. Block. Disarm. Again, Suki. No, Bekko, hold the stick correctly. Again. Suki, never mind your fingers. You are fine. Pain is a great teacher.'*

'Not all learning has to be fun, Suki,' Kuma reminded her severely. 'Sometimes you do need to repeat things and work hard. You know that! And I'm sure you're improving. Master Tak does seem to be a good teacher. He's really skilful and patient. Isn't he, Bekko?'

Bekko sighed gloomily. He was struggling with the stick work even more than Suki. But he always tried to be fair. 'He is very skilful, and I know we are only beginners. Kang and Nita are much better than us, and they think he's brilliant. I do feel like I'm making such slow progress though, Kuma.'

'Well, they have been cadets a lot longer than you, so that's only to be expected. And slow progress is still progress!' Kuma said sternly. 'You love a challenge.' They nodded obediently. Warrior Monkeys always tried to focus on the positives.

Just then there was a loud knocking on the gate. They looked at each other in surprise. Unexpected visitors to Senshi Castle were very rare.

'Who could it be?' Bekko asked Kuma, who looked as surprised as they were.

'I don't know,' he replied, already putting on his helmet and heading down to investigate. 'I haven't been told to prepare for any guests. Stay there.' They did as they were told, knowing it was his job to monitor visitors alone. However, Suki couldn't resist climbing up on the window seat to look down to the outside of the gate.

'Who is it?' Bekko asked, curiously, seeing her eyebrows raised.

'Come and see!' she answered with a mixture of amusement and fascination on her face. 'I've never seen anything like it before!'

Bekko jumped up next to her. Below them, a medium-sized creature turned and waved up at them with a cheerful smile. He had black and white stripes like a raccoon but was the shape of a fox, with a long nose and ears. What made him look so comical was his purple hat (set at a jaunty angle) and his fancy silk waistcoat, which was joined with gold buttons. To complete the picture, he held a shiny black and white cane and a small brown suitcase. He seemed extremely happy and excited to see them.

They could see him introducing himself to Kuma, who had opened the top part of the gate to check who was ringing the bell. The stranger removed his hat, performing a very elaborate bow with a flowery wave of his arms. Kuma was speaking to him, but they couldn't hear what was said. Then the guard bear closed the top of the gate and withdrew. The stranger settled himself to wait, sitting on his little suitcase with a smile.

Suki and Bekko jumped down to meet Kuma. 'Who is it?' they demanded. 'He looks so friendly and funny! Where is he from?'

'He says he is a tanuki from Gimandesh,' Kuma explained. 'His name is Loko. He is asking to meet Sensei Rika. He seems very friendly and polite, but I have asked him to wait while we let Sensei Rika know he is here. Would you two run and tell her, please?'

He didn't need to ask twice. They bounded down the stairs and hurried to find Sensei Rika. It didn't take long: she was walking in the kitchen courtyard with Master Chan. They both looked rather taken aback to hear the news.

'Black and white? Like a fox? With a . . . hat?' Rika repeated their words to ensure she had heard correctly.

'Hmmm, Rika. That sounds like one of the tanuki of northern Gimandesh,' Chan commented, raising an eyebrow.

Suki burst in. 'Yes! Kuma said he was a tanuki. I've never heard of them. Have you met one before?'

Chan shook his head. 'I know a little

about them, but I have never met one. Extraordinary creatures. I wonder what brings him here?'

'Shall we invite him in?' Rika asked him. 'I confess I am intrigued to know what he could want.'

Chan nodded. 'I think it is worth hearing him at any rate. Would you like me to join you?'

'Definitely,' she replied. 'Cadets, could you escort our visitor to the council room? We will meet him there. I'll ask Fara to bring some tea.'

Loko danced inside the gate when Kuma opened it. He seemed barely able to contain his joy. He bowed to Bekko and

Suki. Then he bowed to Kuma again. Then he skipped along next to his guides as they took him to the council room. He was full of admiration for the castle as they passed through the main courtyard and past the training hall where some of the younger students were sweeping the floor. Suki and Bekko stood at the edge of the council room and bowed before introducing their guest.

Chan and Rika rose to their feet to welcome the newcomer. 'Welcome to Senshi Castle,' Sensei Rika said, with a courteous bow. 'I am Rika, Guardian of Senshi. This is Master Chan, one of our respected elders.'

The tanuki first bowed elegantly,

then turned a somersault of excitement. 'I am Loko of the Gimandeshi Tanuki. I am deeply honoured to make your acquaintance.'

Bekko thought he saw Sensei Rika look slightly annoyed by the somersaulting, but she mastered her feelings quickly and invited the tanuki to sit down and take some tea. Tradition taught that she must not immediately ask why he was there. In his turn, he accepted the tea she poured for him and sipped it delicately.

'What delicious tea!' he exclaimed. 'Is it grown here on the islands?'

'I'm glad it's to your taste,' Sensei Rika replied. 'Yes, we grow our own tea on Jindo. Only enough for the islanders

though; we don't sell it abroad. Our plantations are very small.'

'Ah, that would be why I've never had the pleasure of drinking it before. This is my first visit to the Shanti Islands, though I have heard much about what an impressive community you have here.' Loko spread his hands as he spoke, indicating wonder at his surroundings. 'I saw many student warriors in the grounds as well. A powerful little army!'

Chan put out a firm hand to explain— or was it to correct?—this idea. 'We learn to fight so that we never need to fight. Although our warriors are strong, their energy is always directed to maintaining peace and justice here. Few know about our islands, but those who do understand that we seek only to be left to rule ourselves quietly.'

'We learn to fight so that we never need to fight,' repeated Loko slowly. 'I see. You mean that no one will attack you because you are strong?'

'Not quite. Perhaps our young warriors should explain. Bekko? Suki?' Chan beckoned them forwards.

'We learn discipline and control,' began Bekko, clearly. Suki continued, and they took it in turns.

'We learn justice and kindness.'

'We learn the value of effort. This makes us respectful and supportive of each other.'

'We don't need to prove ourselves with

fighting because we know ourselves.'

'And, as a community, we share our strengths instead of wasting them by competing with each other.'

'Magnificent! What a splendid philosophy. I would love to learn more about it.' Loko did seem absolutely fascinated by their explanation. 'In fact,' he continued, 'I would like to learn with these excellent students, if you will allow me.'

Sensei Rika leaned forwards, eyebrows raised. 'To learn with us?' she asked.

'Yes! In my country there is no peace. Villages fight. Everyone wants to control the river towns, but no one agrees who should be in charge. It seems as if there is always a new ruler with magic powers, but once they get comfortable another battle breaks out. Only the strongest can rule, but no one is strong for long if their talismans are stolen.' Loko shook his head sorrowfully.

'We have heard similar accounts from other visitors,' Rika said seriously. 'However, we do not involve ourselves in the troubles of other countries.'

'Yes, I understand that. And I never thought things could be different. I thought that was just how people lived. But I heard about the Shanti Islands from sea traders who have passed through. It sounded like paradise! I wanted to come and see for myself. So here I am. I can hardly believe it!' Loko took another sip of his tea and sighed with happiness.

'Tell us more about yourself. We have never had a tanuki here before,' Chan said, exchanging a glance with Rika.

'There's nothing important to tell, really! We are fun-loving animals who like to learn and make new friends.'

Rika smiled politely and poured a little more tea. Suki and Bekko could tell that she was unconvinced by the visitor's words.

'Come now,' Chan murmured. 'Tanuki are not simply lovers of fun and adventure. You have some special skills, isn't that true?'

Was that irritation on the tanuki's face? It was fleeting and rapidly replaced with a hearty eruption of laughter. 'I see our reputation goes before us! I imagine you are referring to this?' And with a sudden wriggle, the creature . . . melted! And from the puddle of black and white on the floor emerged a sniggering weasel. But before Suki and Bekko could get over their surprise, the weasel also melted and was replaced by a small black and white tree. It still had Loko's hat delicately balanced on one of its high branches and seemed to be quivering with amusement.

'How can a tree laugh?' Suki whispered to Bekko in astonishment.

'Erm, surely you should be asking how a tanuki can turn into a tree?' Bekko whispered back, evidently very disturbed by what they were seeing.

There was a giant mouse; a small black and white giraffe; a vase of flowers; then finally Loko reappeared as a tanuki. He bowed and gave himself an enthusiastic round of applause, still giggling. Rika was also clapping, but her tone was very dry.

'Nice party trick,' she observed. 'Does it feel uncomfortable to perform?'

'Oh no! I'm used to it! I just get a bit tired if I do too many all in one go. It's only a bit of fun.'

'Fun? Deception and disguise more like!' Bekko muttered to Suki, who had enjoyed the little display. They had been sent to ask Fara to prepare a room for the guest and were avidly discussing what they had seen. 'I don't like it, Suki,' said Bekko. 'How can you trust someone who changes all the time?'

Suki shrugged. 'He's just showing us what he can do. Imagine if he didn't show us that he had magical powers. At least he isn't trying to hide it.'

'But Sensei always says we shouldn't think of magic as something fun. I don't think she likes it much either.' Bekko was quite right: Sensei Rika had looked more serious than amused, even though she had snapped herself into a gracious smile when Loko had shifted back to his normal shape. Was this visitor harmless, or was there trouble brewing at Senshi?

CHAPTER FOUR

The next morning, Suki was in the gatehouse wriggling in the chair as Kuma tried to tame her hair.

'I think we're going to need a few more grips, Suki-su,' he sighed. 'It just keeps bouncing out again.'

'Whatever it takes. Master Tak is so fierce! Can't we just glue it down?' she asked, doing her best not to fidget. She was always so energetic; sitting still was one of her biggest challenges.

'Ha! I don't think that would be very comfortable,' he laughed. 'Nearly done, anyway. Just try not to do too many headstands on your way to find Bekko! Train hard, Suki, and see you later.'

Suki dashed out of the gatehouse and raced off to the water garden to meet Bekko as she did every morning. She slowed down as she approached so that she didn't disturb his work.

The water garden was tranquil and beautiful; the only sounds were the trickle of the waterfall and a calm, continuous voice. It was Bekko's. He seemed to be talking to the stream, but Suki knew there was someone else

around. Ah, there he was. Limping painfully, a giant dog edged towards the water. Bekko looked away gently in order to give the nervous creature the confidence to drink. But he kept up his soft encouragement, knowing the dog liked to hear a reassuring voice nearby.

Bekko knew what it was like to feel lonely. Although the castle was full of young warriors, Suki was his only real friend. She didn't care that he was different; didn't care if he talked endlessly about boats, stones, or the history of famous warriors. She knew he didn't like to hang out with the other monkeys and often found it hard to talk to them. She was always ready to stand up for him if the others were mean. When she wasn't around, he sometimes felt like he didn't really fit in. Perhaps that was why he was so determined to help the dog that no one liked.

He had named it Ishi, and although no one said it was Bekko's dog, they all knew he was the only one who could get near him. At first, Ishi would snarl at everyone. He refused food. He wouldn't let anyone touch his injured leg—broken when his selfish master Jirugi had thrown him violently into a fight to save himself. Jirugi had escaped, and Ishi had been left behind. And so began his new life at Senshi Castle.

Bekko believed that Ishi had never

been treated kindly or felt a friendly hand. Although he wanted to hug Ishi to make him feel like he had a friend, he could tell that Ishi was much too scared to let anyone close. Gaining the dog's trust became Bekko's long and patient mission.

Recently, his patience had been rewarded when Ishi started to follow him. He would always retreat if Bekko tried to get close so Bekko learned to pretend not to see him. The other monkeys got used to seeing Bekko with Ishi walking behind him like a separated shadow, but they remained afraid and suspicious of the dog, especially as he would growl at them loudly, showing his big sharp teeth.

No one wanted to get to know him any better, and many of the other students thought Bekko was strange for wasting so much time with an unfriendly beast.

This morning, a few of the warrior students were looking over the wall into the water garden. Nita was one of the older cadet students. She disliked Bekko and found Ishi very alarming.

'Honestly,' she grumbled to Kang, the baboon who was the biggest cadet. 'It's dangerous having that thing around. It looks like it wants to eat us. I think Sensei Rika should have left it far away in the woods.' Nita was quite brave about giving her opinion when their teachers were not around. She would never dare to challenge them face-to-face though!

'Doesn't bother me.' Kang was known for his lack of sympathy. 'Bekko is already weird enough. Stops him bugging the rest of us, and hey, if anyone gets eaten it will probably be him.' That made Nita snigger. Yash, Kang's best friend, also laughed nastily.

'Better not let Suki hear you moan about her friend,' he warned Kang. 'She can't take a joke if it is about Bekko. Where is she anyway? Stuck up a big tree somewhere?'

Nita sighed. 'Here she comes. Must have been getting Kuma to sort out her haystack hair. Master Tak was not impressed with her last week. So messy!

I don't know why she and Bekko were
given their red belts!'

'Well, they did save us all from Jirugi
and that volcano thing,' Kang pointed
out.

'Did they, though?' Nita sneered.
'Seems very exaggerated to me. They
were probably just lucky to be there
when Sensei Rika and Master Chan got

rid of Jirugi and his helpers. Apart from that horrible dog!'

Kang raised an eyebrow at Yash, and they both shrugged. It was pointless arguing with Nita. She seemed to be jealous and resentful of the attention Suki and Bekko had received for their actions. And while Kang was not especially fond of the two young cadets, he didn't begrudge them the praise they had earned. He'd had enough standing around anyway.

'Come on,' he said to Yash. 'Let's go and work on our pair drills before class.' They ran to the training hall, followed by a grumpy Nita.

Meanwhile, Suki walked quietly into

the edge of the garden to let Bekko know it was time for class. He began to move backwards slowly.

'Good boy, Ishi, see you later, boy. You have a good run this morning and I'll come and find you at lunchtime, hey?' he said, warmly and calmly. Ishi dropped his head down between his paws, looking sad that Bekko was going, but knowing this was the normal daily routine. But then he flinched, growled viciously, and stood snarling.

'What happened?' Suki asked, though she could see from Bekko's distressed face that he didn't know what had upset Ishi. Then they both heard voices. Firstly Loko's chattering voice . . . who was he talking to?

'Fascinating! So you're a master of stick fighting? That's just so amazing! I wish I knew how to fight properly!' Bekko was watching Ishi, whose hackles were raised as Loko came into view with his companion. It was Master Tak. He looked impatient and busy.

'I must get ready for class now. Please excuse me,' he said, trying to get rid of the little tanuki who was pestering him with questions.

'Can't I come along though? I promise I won't be any trouble,' pleaded Loko.

'I'm sorry, I cannot teach you these skills. It would be dangerous to teach someone who is not already trained in the foundations of martial arts.' Master Tak was dismissive, but Loko wasn't ready to give up just yet.

'Are you worried I might get hurt? I don't mind that!' he assured the stern-faced teacher.

'No. I'm more worried you would hurt someone else!' Tak replied, severely. 'In untrained hands a stick is very dangerous. You have to respect the self-control and the discipline of the arts, Loko. One does not simply pick up a stick and start hitting things. That's violence. If you're truly here to learn the way of the Warrior Monkeys, then you must accept the difference between training and dangerous play. I don't think you get it yet.'

Loko looked offended. 'Just because you've been here longer than me you think you know everything! I'm a pretty fast learner, you know!'

'It's not my decision. You're not a warrior cadet. The class is not for you. That is all. Now look out for that dog. He doesn't like me. Looks like he doesn't like you either!'

Indeed, Ishi's growling had become quite scary, and Suki was worried he would actually attack.

Then she heard Loko laughing. 'I'm not scared of dogs. I know loads of dogs like that. It's easy for me to get rid of them. They don't like it if I do this . . .' and he morphed into a dog just like Ishi himself. Although he looked ridiculous with his little hat still perched on his head, there was no doubt the sudden appearance of another dog was upsetting to Ishi, who dropped to the ground and whined unhappily. Loko became himself once more, still laughing. 'And there's one creature these dogs really don't like!' he continued, rapidly changing into a mandrill. Although nowhere near as large as Jirugi, the resemblance was still incredible. Ishi jumped out of his skin, turned tail, and ran away howling. Bekko and Suki looked at each other in shock; then Bekko immediately ran after his dog. Suki hesitated. She wanted to go after Bekko, but behind her she could hear Tak furiously berating Loko.

'Are you insane? Don't you know that Jirugi is the mortal enemy of the Warrior Monkeys? What do you think Sensei Rika would think if she saw you making a joke out of something so serious? You'll get yourself thrown out!'

Loko was looking sorrowful. 'I'm sorry. It was only a bit of fun! I won't do it again.'

'You'd better not! Now, get out of my way. I have a class to teach!' Master Tak brushed the visitor aside and strode off to the training hall. Suki watched as Loko picked himself up and straightened his hat with an expression of irritation. Then she realized she needed to grab Bekko as quickly as possible so they were not late to class. Shaking off the angry urge to question Loko, she zoomed out of the garden to find her friend.

CHAPTER FIVE

Bekko had not managed to find Ishi and was very anxious about him. He took that anxiety with him into the class. Even on a good day, he found stick training challenging. Today was not a good day.

Master Tak was a forceful and tough teacher. His stick skills were superb; he taught clearly and with enthusiasm, but his class knew not to test his patience. He always had a reason not to be sympathetic. Bashed fingers? Defend better! Feeling tired? Great opportunity for testing discipline! Suki had once made the mistake of forgetting what had been taught in the previous lesson. Master Tak had made her stay after class and do the technique one hundred times to make up for failing to practise between classes. She had never skipped her homework again.

On one hand, Bekko liked how strict and simple the lessons were. He liked routine and rules, so the constant drilling and repetition helped him to feel settled. He was sensitive to the noise of constantly clashing sticks though, and he liked to stuff some cotton wool in his ears before pair drills.

As they entered the hall, Yash and Kang were practising an attack-and-disarm drill from the previous class. Nita and Lili were warming up their wrists, their sticks rotating up and down swiftly. Suki and Bekko took out their sticks and also began the warm-up drills while admiring Kang and Yash's pair work.

'Look how smoothly Yash defends!' Bekko whispered to Suki as Kang stepped in to swing his stick hard at Yash's head; Yash deflected the stick with his own, then wove around Kang's weapon to force it out of his hand.

'I know!' Suki muttered back. 'It looks so easy. But how is he managing to use Kang's power against him like that? I keep thinking he is going to get bashed, but it doesn't happen.'

'Look, now they are doing it the other way. Even Kang looks graceful and balanced!' Bekko usually expected Kang to use just physical force, but there was no doubt he was moving lightly and dodging with finesse.

'I don't see much point in that though,' Suki shrugged. 'Kang is the biggest and the strongest. If he resisted Yash with his power, then he would just win every time.'

Bekko frowned at her.

'But, Suki, there is always someone stronger, or cleverer, or more agile. What if Kang has to fight Jirugi one day?'

From behind them a light but firm voice spoke up.

'Bekko is right. But also not right. To compare yourself to another is not in the warrior spirit. You must always compare yourself to one person only!'

Suki turned to Master Tak and bowed, before bursting into her question.

'Who, sir? Who must we compare ourselves to? Is it you? Sensei Rika? Master Chan?'

He shook his head.

'No, Suki. There is only one you must surpass. It is the Suki of yesterday. And tomorrow's Suki should be smarter, stronger, and braver than today's. Line up, class! Let us begin.'

Inspired by Kang and Yash's work, Suki worked extra hard through class. However, she began to get a little frustrated when she felt she was getting better at the defence but Bekko was still 'attacking' quite gently.

'Really try and hit me!' she encouraged him.

'I'm worried it will hurt you,' he said, unhappily. 'It doesn't feel right trying to whack you over the head.'

'But that's the only way I will learn to defend myself! No one is going to try and attack me like you just did. Not unless they are trying to splat me with a banana.'

Bekko's anxiety was becoming overpowering. He felt uncomfortable and awkward with the drill. He was worried about Ishi vanishing. He felt totally out of his depth, as if he had never trained before. Suki was losing patience, so he took a deep breath and tried again. This time he managed to bring the stick down with more force, but instead of targeting her head, the stick swished down past her shoulder, and so her blocking move was completely unnecessary and she was defending against nothing. Master Tak took this moment to call the class to the mat. He pulled up a box of old sticks and perched on the edge to talk to them.

'To know your enemy, you must

BECOME your enemy.' The class all nodded; this was an idea they had to learn in Sensei Rika's class. He studied their faces. 'What does this mean? Yash, what do you think?'

'Well, sir, it means we have to learn how the enemy fights.'

Nita put her hand up. 'Sir, doesn't it also mean we have to learn how the enemy thinks? Because if you understand, then you can guess what they will do next?'

'That's true, Nita,' Master Tak agreed, though they could tell by his voice that this was not the whole answer. He waited for them to think some more, and a silence fell over the class as they tried to figure it out. He never rushed to help them answer questions; he believed that deep thinking was a necessary exercise for the brain.

Kang raised a hand. 'Is part of it about trying to test each other under pressure, sir?' He had been training with Tak long enough to know how much emphasis his teacher placed on defending against sudden, strong attacks, so he felt this was a safe guess.

'If your defence doesn't work under pressure, then it is no defence. It is a false security.' Tak stood up and paced up and down the hall, getting increasingly energetic in his words. 'If your partner does not help you test your defences, then they put you in danger. Bekko, your strike missed Suki. Why?'

Bekko was confused and upset. He found it hard to look up and impossible to talk. He tried to cough to clear his throat but just ended up shrugging. Suki knew he was upset, but also knew that to Master Tak it would look like Bekko was sulking.

'Cadet, you must protect your partner. So you must attack her. If you do not become her enemy, she will not learn to defend herself effectively. You are failing her. Do you understand?' Master Tak was very stern. Bekko just wished he could hide away. There was no way he could explain his thoughts to Tak. He ended up shrugging again, which clearly annoyed his teacher. Bekko didn't dare look up. He imagined everyone staring at him with disgust. The worst training partner in the room. Probably shouldn't even be a cadet. There was silence for a moment, thankfully broken by Lili.

'Sir?' she said. 'Could you help me with my stances on the defence side?' Suki shot her a grateful look as the focus of the room moved away from Bekko and Master Tak went through the foot movements for the drill.

Battling the urge to simply run out of the training hall, Bekko tried to calm himself down with some deep breaths. When, finally, the lesson finished, he bowed out quickly, avoiding everyone.

'Are you going after him?' Lili asked Suki, seeing her hovering by the door, watching as Bekko ran off.

Suki turned to her, grateful that she was not the only one to see her friend was upset. 'I think he wants to be alone. I don't want to make him feel worse,' she explained. 'I will find him a bit later when he's had some time on his own.'

Lili smiled sympathetically. 'You're a good friend to him, Suki. He's lucky to have you.'

'Actually, Lili, I'm the lucky one,' Suki said immediately. 'Bekko is the kindest and bravest friend anyone could have. I don't think Master Tak understands him yet. When he gets upset, it doesn't

help to put him under more pressure. He
needs time to think things through. I'll
find him after lunch.'

Senshi Castle's gardens were extensive
and very beautiful. They were divided
by streams and intricate arrangements
of trees and bushes. Today, Bekko took
himself to the Zen garden, where light-
coloured stones made patterns on the
ground. He liked the peace and the
privacy. He had a smooth pebble in his
own pocket; he took it out and rubbed
his thumb across the surface while he
thought. Gradually he became aware that
he was not alone. Ishi had reappeared
and was lurking behind some ornamental

bushes about ten metres away. Relieved beyond measure, Bekko chirruped to him gently, and the dog lay down under the bushes, watching Bekko. Although Bekko would have liked Ishi to come closer, he was simply delighted to see him again. It felt like one part of his anxiety faded away. Then the quietness of the garden and the feel of the warm stone in his hand made it easier for him to think about what was going wrong in class.

He absolutely understood the importance of using powerful attacks for training. When it was just kicking and punching, he was used to finding the right level of force, although it wasn't easy for him. However, using weapons was a whole new challenge. He tried to understand his own feelings: there was deep confusion and discomfort. And fear. There was definitely fear. What was he afraid of?

He wasn't aware of time passing. It was noise that brought him out of his meditation. Humming softly, Chan entered the garden with a rake over his shoulder. His tread was light on the gravel path; to Bekko he seemed to float along like a spirit rather than crunching the stones as he arrived. His long, flowing hair added to the ethereal feel of his presence. He did not seem surprised to see Bekko. But then he rarely seemed surprised by anything. Once he had been the head of Senshi Castle, head of all the Shanti Islands. Now he spent his days tending and nurturing the gardens and keeping an eye on the young students as they trained.

'What brings you here, Bekko?' he asked, as he began to rake the stones into a new pattern.

'Good afternoon, sir,' Bekko bowed respectfully. 'I was having some trouble in my weapons class. So I came here to think.'

Chan continued to rake. The gravel took on symmetrical swirls as the rhythmic movements shifted the stones. It was mesmerizing to see the straight lines turning into crescents, and the

crescents linking together to make a chain-like pattern across the garden.

Finding it soothing to watch the new patterns in the ground, Bekko organized his thoughts a little more.

'Master Tak tells us we must be like the enemy,' he told Chan. 'Otherwise we can't learn to defend. But if I become the enemy, what if I can't go back to being me again? Maybe it will change me. Master Chan, I don't want to be cruel. What if I enjoy being powerful? Being mean? I do get angry. It's hard to control my feelings. I'm scared, sir.'

He felt relieved to have been able to put his fear into words. Chan finished the edge of his pattern slowly. Turning towards Bekko, he leaned on his rake and looked at him with compassion and wisdom.

'Do I believe you will lose control? No, I don't. Can I promise that? No, I can't. No one can. We live in a world where you will need to defend yourself and your friends, Bekko. I hope it will not always be as hard for you as it has been for us. I can't promise that either.' Chan turned back to the gravel to begin the next part of his pattern.

Bekko was disappointed that Chan had no simple answer for him. But, of course, the wise gardener had not finished.

'When you worry about the balance of power and control; when you constantly check your partners to see if you are challenging them, not bullying them; when your happiness isn't based on your own success . . . these show you that you have not lost your warrior heart.'

'Sir? What happened with Jirugi?' Bekko's voice was very timid, knowing the subject of Jirugi was a painful one for his old teacher.

'Jirugi was blessed with incredible strength. Fighting came easily to him. He did not really feel what it was like to be weak, and so I believe he never developed respect for weaker students.' Finally, the patterns in the path seemed complete and Chan turned around.

'Perhaps one day he will see that

kindness is the greatest power of all.
I never stop hoping, Bekko. And here
comes another kind warrior. I think she's
been worried about you.'

Chan bowed to Bekko, swept his
hair back, and left as quietly as he had
arrived. By contrast, Suki could be heard
calling 'Bekko! Bekko!' She burst into
the garden like a mini tornado. Under his
bush, Ishi jumped, but when he saw Suki
he didn't run away.

'Oh, there you are, Bekko!' she
exclaimed, looking pleased and relieved.
'I brought you some lunch from Fara.
Are you hungry?'

'Really, really hungry!' he smiled,
suddenly realizing how long it had been

since breakfast. He took a bundle of nuts and banana bread from Suki, and they sat together while he ate.

Suki looked across the little garden. 'Wow, look at the gravel! It's Senshi Island! How cool is that?'

'Really?' Bekko raised his eyebrows. 'I don't see it.'

'Sure it is!' Suki leapt up and scampered down to the design. 'Look here: these swirls around the edge are the sea. These square bits look like the castle up here. This looks like the mountains down here. Don't you think so?'

'I think you're right!' he said, thoughtfully. 'But the island isn't quite that shape in real life. Does it look like a heart to you? See how the waves cut in at the top there?'

'Ah yes! Senshi means warrior, so this is a warrior heart. Brilliant. Chan is so clever with his patterns. I wonder when he did this one?' Suki danced round the edge of the gravel, careful not to disturb it.

'He was here, Suki. I was talking to him while he did it, but I didn't notice the picture. Let's go and see Kuma, shall we? I'll tell you about this morning as well. I think I know why I was having trouble with the drills. And what on earth was Loko doing, scaring Ishi like that? I really don't like him!'

'Me neither!' Suki agreed. 'We need to keep an eye on him. I definitely don't trust him any more!'

They headed past the ornamental garden, chatting together, followed by a slinking Ishi. All three were framed in Chan's contemplative gaze as he tended his growing plants.

CHAPTER SIX

All the students had to take turns to help
prepare food for everyone in the castle,
and the next morning it was time for
Suki and Bekko to join the team to help
with lunch. Chaos in the Senshi kitchen
was not unusual because Fara was a loud,
busy sort of dragon who liked to shout
instructions and throw things around.
But when Suki and Bekko arrived, they
found Fara was not the loudest person in

the kitchen any more.

It appeared that Loko had taken over
the cooking for the day. Fara sat in
the corner while Loko entertained the
students with his antics. One minute
he was chopping several carrots at once
while in the shape of an octopus. The
next minute he was a stork, flapping
across the room to drop vegetables
into the boiling pots on the stove. Each
transformation was greeted with laughter
and applause from Nita, Yash, and little
Ko, who were supposed to be shelling
prawns and chopping onions.

Suki began to unpack a big crate of
bananas. Bekko sat with her skinning,
chopping, and skewering them for Fara.

They watched together as Loko became a little elephant, stamping on walnuts to crack them for the others. Trumpeting and dancing, with an enthusiastic audience, the visitor was unaware of Suki and Bekko's unimpressed faces on the sidelines.

'Fara, do you think Loko is careless with magic?' Suki asked, knowing that Fara was always very blunt in her opinions and would not hide her thoughts.

'Careless?' Fara repeated, pushing her glasses up her nose. 'Irresponsible, more like. I don't know what Rika is thinking, having that tanuki running around here with his daft behaviour. Magic messes up minds. One person with unbalanced powers is a danger to everyone else!'

Bekko looked surprised at Fara's words. Suki thought that perhaps Fara was being too dramatic.

'Maybe he isn't doing any harm? He seems to be just trying to make everyone laugh, doesn't he?' she asked, wanting Fara to say more.

Fara was very ready to say more. 'Seems to be? Seems to be? I know what *seems* to be happening, but who knows what's really going on? A creature like that could be a spy. He could be here to cause all sorts of trouble. I don't trust him. I told Rika so myself.'

'What did she say?' Bekko asked, curiously. If he and Suki were suspicious, and Fara was suspicious too, surely Sensei Rika must be as well?

'She just told me to be patient. "Time will tell, Fara," she said. I mean, I get that we are supposed to welcome guests and share our ideas. Look at Master Tak: he's sharing his knowledge and learning from us in return. That's a balance. This Loko just seems to be here to make trouble.'

Fara frowned again, took a deep breath, and began to flame the fritters. Across the kitchen, a play fight had erupted. Loko-the-elephant and Yash were shooting chickpeas at Ko while Nita hid behind the table. Bekko couldn't see what she was doing, but suddenly she leapt out in front of the barrage of peas, holding up a string of noodles tied around a radish. 'Behold! The Kokoro medal! You cannot harm us, evil elephant!'

'Ah! You win!' laughed Yash, dropping

his chickpeas.

Loko resumed his normal shape, looking confused. 'What? Why? I don't get it! That's not fair!'

Yash shrugged. 'The Kokoro medal is the ultimate protection. We can't harm them now.'

Nita and Ko had started clearing up the mess, aware that Fara was tapping her foot, arms folded, glasses firmly pushed up her long nose. But Loko wasn't giving up that easily. 'I thought you were warriors, not wizards. I don't believe you have a protective medal. Where is it?'

'Hardly anyone knows. It's too dangerous: what if it was stolen? It is the heart of the warrior; we'd be powerless without it!' Nita loved to be dramatic, and there was no doubt she had everyone's full attention. Especially little Ko, who looked very scared.

'Powerless?' he said in a wobbly voice. 'But why do we learn to fight if we really depend on magic to protect us?'

'Don't listen to her.' Yash pushed Nita and her opinion to one side. 'We are very strong, but the medal also helps protect us all here in Senshi Castle. I've heard the ancient warriors leave their power in the medal when they die. That's why I think it is kept in the gardens, where the old warriors have their statues.'

'That's rubbish. It's in a secret place under the castle, where all the magic is kept!' Nita didn't want Yash to get all the attention.

'Under the castle?' Loko leaned forwards eagerly. 'Where?'

'Well, duh! It's a secret!' Nita replied, laughing.

'You shouldn't talk about these things as a joke!' Bekko burst out, unable to listen any more. Everyone looked at him in surprise.

'Oh, shut up, Bekko!' Nita snapped. 'You think you're so special. No one cares how much you suck up to Sensei Rika. Bet you think you know all the secrets of Senshi. Well, here's a secret for you—you're still just a weirdo. You and your stupid dog.'

'Take. That. Back.' Suki leapt across the room and confronted Nita. Nita didn't flinch.

'Oooooh, scary Suki too! Not everyone wants to be teacher's pet, you know. Lighten up, the pair of you.'

Fara bustled over rapidly and quickly separated Nita and Suki before things got worse. 'Time to get this kitchen cleaned up!' she bellowed. 'Neat and tidy; organized and disciplined! Hurry up now!'

Bekko was really upset by Nita's cruel words. Suki, on the other hand, was more worried by Loko's interest in the medal. It was time to look for Sensei Rika.

Bekko and Suki found Rika whirling weapons in the castle grounds. Priya, her guard bear, had a bucket full of chestnuts and was throwing them at Rika. Rika's nunchucks were just a blur as chestnuts fell from the air around her, smashed to pieces. When she saw the students approaching, Rika halted the practice and bowed to Priya in thanks for her help.

'Could we talk to you, Sensei, please?' Suki asked. Priya began to collect her bucket to give them some privacy, but Rika motioned for her to stay.

'Sure. Is everything OK?' she asked, sitting cross-legged on the ground and inviting them to do the same.

'Well, yes,' began Bekko uncertainly.

'And, maybe no . . .' continued Suki, seeing Bekko was nervous about making accusations about Loko without any evidence. He had been reluctant to come with Suki. However, she felt his opinion was also important, so she had persuaded him to join her.

Suki wasted no time. 'We think Loko might be a spy. He's been asking a lot of questions, and it doesn't feel right. Also, he was mean to Bekko's dog.'

'To Ishi?' Sensei Rika was surprised. 'How?'

Bekko explained what had happened, and how scared Ishi had been. 'I know it could be just a coincidence, but what if Loko is one of Jirugi's spies? That would explain why he imitated a mandrill.'

'And also, deliberately scaring an animal is just wrong,' Suki stated firmly. 'I was prepared to give him a fair chance when he arrived, but he thought it was funny to upset that poor creature. That's not the action of someone I can trust.'

'Different cultures may not have the same respect for other creatures, Suki. I agree with you, but it doesn't necessarily mean he's evil.' Rika sighed, looking concerned. 'However, we have been hearing rumours about a possible attack by Jirugi. I had a message from Silla about reports from sea traders who claim to have seen a mandrill travelling this way. Chan and I are going over to meet with the other guardians this afternoon. We're aware Loko might be more than he seems. You two need to keep a close eye on him while I'm away.'

One was thrilled to have the task of spying on the potential spy. The other was terrified of the responsibility. Both were determined to do their very best. Bekko found his voice. 'We won't let you down, Sensei.' They bowed farewell and set off across the lawn to look for Loko.

CHAPTER SEVEN

Loko was so loud and silly that it wasn't
too difficult to keep an eye on him.
Through the afternoon, he played with
the student monkeys in the yard. He
joined in with Lili's skipping game: as a
kangaroo; then as a rope. Suki and Bekko
noticed that he seemed to stay especially
near Nita.

'Do you think it's because she talks a
lot?' Bekko whispered to Suki, as once

more Loko asked Nita questions about the history of the castle, claiming to be fascinated by secrets.

'I'm sure it is,' Suki replied. 'I also heard him asking Ko the same questions. Ko is too young to be suspicious of him. But I don't think either of them really knows anything about the vault.'

When night fell, however, Suki and Bekko were less sure what to do. They sat in the dark garden, Ishi close by, and discussed their options. 'If he tries to get down in the vault, he won't find the entrance. And he can't do it on his own anyway. Maybe we should just sleep now and watch him again tomorrow until Sensei Rika gets back?' Suki suggested.

'I don't know, Suki.' Bekko had one of his stones in his hand, turning it over and over without even noticing it. 'What if he tries to leave the castle?'

'We should follow him, if he goes,' she replied. 'But Kuma would notice if he went out?'

'Don't be silly!' said Bekko. 'He's a shape-shifter! He's not going to walk through the gate! He'd probably dig under the walls. Or fly over the top. Or . . .'

'Or slither like a really big snake with a stupid hat on?' Half shocked, half amused, Suki pointed at a long black and white (slightly fluffy) snake, which was making its way towards the castle walls.

'Wow, that is one dumb disguise,'

Bekko giggled. It was hard to take Loko seriously even though they didn't trust him. 'Come on, let's run. If we go through the gate, we can catch up with him while he swims through the moat.'

Kuma knew they had been asked to watch Loko, and though he was anxious about letting them go outside the castle, he also knew that he was not the best choice for a sneaky mission.

'If there's any trouble, we will come straight back to get you!' Suki promised over her shoulder as she sped through the gatehouse. Bekko was already running silently along the outer wall. It was not difficult to find Loko. Once over the wall, he had transformed back into his regular body and was humming and skipping his way into the forest. Suki and Bekko climbed well out of sight up to the branches, hopping discreetly from tree to tree, even though it did not seem as if Loko had any concerns that he might not be alone. But he was not alone for long. Ahead of them, a worried-looking snub-nosed monkey was sitting on a boulder. He leapt up immediately when he saw Loko approaching.

'Loko! There you are! You're late. Lord Jirugi will be very annoyed!'

Suki and Bekko froze, concealed in the forest's canopy of leaves. Now Suki slid quietly down alongside Bekko, and they exchanged alarmed faces. Jirugi. So close to Senshi!

'No way Rika and Chan would have left if they knew Jirugi was this close!' Bekko breathed in Suki's ear, echoing the exact thought that was in her head.

Loko didn't seem to be very concerned with what the little monkey had said. 'He's always very annoyed, Yunnan. Probably your fault. I'd be annoyed if I had to hang around with you.'

'No need to be rude,' Yunnan protested. 'I'm doing my best! It isn't easy to serve my master and keep him happy. A different tree every night instead of his own apartment. Nowhere to make the tea. Always hiding . . . I hope we can get this medal soon and go home!

Have you figured out where it is yet?'

'No, not yet. These Warrior Monkeys don't just leave stuff lying around, you know! I've definitely gained their trust. I expect they will soon tell me,' Loko said airily. 'Anyway, I don't have to explain myself to you. Take me to Lord Jirugi.'

Stealthy progress through the trees kept Suki and Bekko in earshot of Loko and Yunnan. Loko's loud, confident voice changed dramatically, however, once he actually reached Jirugi. Through the leaves, Suki could see him perform an elegant bow and offer a humble greeting to the mandrill, who looked uncomfortable and impatient. Clearly his temper was even worse than usual.

'Camping! Here I am camping out while you are playing games with the Senshi children! Do you not know I am waiting for you to keep your promise? You said it would be easy to find where the medal was kept. You're as useless as Yunnan!'

'Sir, I'm getting close, I know I am,' grovelled Loko, kneeling rapidly. 'Trouble is, the ones who talk don't seem to know, and the ones who know don't seem to talk, if you know what I mean.'

Suki and Bekko knew exactly what he meant; their instinct about him spending time with Nita and Ko seemed correct!

Jirugi was less understanding. 'It's all

just excuses. I'm fed up with you wasting my time now. You promised you could do this quickly. I've had it with servants telling me they need more time. I don't like waiting. Get me into the castle now. I'll just find it myself.'

Loko bowed and skipped. 'Yes, of course, Lord Jirugi. I can do that. How exciting! Are we going now?'

'I need weapons, fool! Yunnan, gather my things from the cave. It's time for you to see where I grew up. Maybe I was never trusted to learn the secrets of Senshi when I was a student, but they won't be able to hide their treasure from me now. I'm going to get that medal. Come on!'

Their voices faded into the distance. Suki looked at Bekko. 'Kuma?' she said. Bekko nodded instantly. 'Kuma,' he said. 'We have to tell him right now! Oh, why are Rika and Chan away tonight? Quick, let's go!'

Breathless, Suki and Bekko knocked on the castle gate. They didn't dare call out, but the gate was opened quickly and they were ushered inside. Not, however, by Kuma, but by Master Tak. He looked very concerned. 'What's happened?' he asked. 'Did you find Loko? Kuma told me where you'd gone.'

'Where is Kuma?' Bekko grabbed Tak's arm urgently. 'Jirugi is coming,

Master Tak! He's on his way!'

Tak looked very surprised. 'Right now? But how does he plan to get in?'

'Loko said he would help him. I don't know, really, but we need to tell Kuma to raise the alarm.' Suki was looking around wildly. 'Where is he?'

Tak gestured towards the castle grounds. 'He went to do a patrol of the walls because Priya is away with Sensei Rika. He asked me to stay here and wait for you. What are you going to do?'

'I think we need to go down and guard the medal, just in case Jirugi gets through. You and Kuma could defend up here, while Bekko and I go to the vault to ensure the medal is safe. What do you think, sir?' Suki felt very agitated. Without Rika, Chan, and Kuma around, she suddenly felt terribly responsible for the safety of the medal, and the Senshi warriors.

Tak considered her question. 'I don't think you and Bekko should go down alone. There's only one way down to the vault?'

'As far as we know, sir,' Bekko replied.

'Well, then, why don't we ask Kuma to come and guard the entrance while we go down together and check all is OK? Loko's plans haven't been brilliant so far, so I think we're probably all perfectly safe.' Master Tak was very calm, despite Suki and Bekko's agitation. Seeing their worried faces, he explained further. 'Loko doesn't know how to get Jirugi into the castle. He doesn't know where the secret passage is. I'm assuming there are also protections and traps before you get to the vault?'

'Yes, they're hard to get past, even if you know what to do,' Suki told him, beginning to see his point. Maybe this danger was not as bad as she thought.

'Well, then, no need to panic. We can go down together. And if you'll feel better to stay down there until the threat is over, or until Sensei Rika returns, then we should do that. Kuma can keep everything under control up here.' Master Tak's plan did seem to make sense.

'Shall we find Kuma and tell him what we're doing?' Bekko asked. 'I'd expect him to be back by now.'

'I'm sure he's just being extra careful,' Master Tak reassured him. 'Let's meet by the entrance—you get extra torches, and I'll make sure Kuma knows what's happening. Give me ten minutes?'

They agreed and left, telling Tak where to find the door in the wall. Their sense of uneasiness hadn't left them as they scurried across the dark lawn. And behind them, Tak smiled to himself. He stepped over the unconscious Kuma hidden behind the castle gate.

'Now, my brave Kuma. You're going to wake up with quite a headache. But

hopefully not for a few hours yet.' He checked the ropes he'd used to tie up the bear, after he had knocked him out. Then he propped open the castle gate. Ten minutes. That should be just enough time to find Lord Jirugi and show him that at least one of his spies could deliver results. Suki and Bekko had given him the chance to lead his master straight to the prize.

CHAPTER EIGHT

'Shouldn't Master Tak be here now?' Suki asked Bekko. 'Should we go without him?' They stood by the open door, torches lit, ready to go.

'I am sure he'll be here in a minute. So will everyone else if Ishi doesn't calm down, though!' Ishi had rushed up to meet them from the garden but was running in circles, yelping and growling. 'Shh, Ishi, you'll wake everyone! It's OK, boy, it's OK!'

But no matter what he said, Ishi remained upset. 'Do you think he's trying to stop us going to the vault?' Suki wondered. 'Perhaps he can smell Jirugi nearby?'

'I really hope not! Oh, here's Master Tak.' Bekko was relieved to see the teacher approaching briskly. Dodging the snarling dog, Tak apologized for keeping them waiting.

'I was just making sure Kuma knew what was happening,' he explained. 'It's all quiet at the gatehouse though.' Of course he didn't explain that it was quiet in the gatehouse because Kuma was captured and unconscious! Even worse, a triumphant Jirugi was lurking in the shadows, ready to follow them to the vault. No wonder Ishi wouldn't calm down!

'Right, sir. You'll need a torch. And take care, these steps are very old. Follow me.' Suki set off, followed closely by Bekko and Tak. At the foot of the staircase, Suki went to light the lamp while Bekko explained the path through the quicksand to Tak, unaware of little Yunnan eavesdropping from the dark staircase.

'Let me just draw that here in the sand.' Tak sketched the symbol in the sand as Bekko had described it, just as Sensei Rika had done for Suki and Bekko. 'Is this right?'

'Yes, that's right. The lamps are here, and here,' Bekko added, making little X marks at the far end of the diagram. 'And the entrance opens just . . . here.'

'I see. Much easier to understand once I see it written down. Ah, here's Suki. Let's go!' Tak knew that once they had passed through the chamber then Yunnan could show Jirugi and Loko his sketch for passing through the quicksand. All he wanted to do now was to usher the young cadets onwards and clear the way for Jirugi to follow them.

Crossing into the tunnels at the far side of the quicksand, he risked a look back once Suki and Bekko were well ahead of him. He could see shadows moving in the flickering light of the big jade lanterns. His plan seemed to be working well so far. Very satisfactory!

Meanwhile, Suki and Bekko were discussing the boulder trap. Once Tak had caught up with them, they explained it to him.

'I think it makes sense for two of us to wait in the alcove, while only one goes ahead to trigger the boulder,' Suki suggested. 'Just in case something goes wrong.'

'Let me go,' volunteered Bekko. 'I remember exactly where Sensei Rika stood to set it off.'

'Sure,' Suki agreed. 'Master Tak, we need to duck in here, sir.'

But something was not right with their plan. Bekko went down the passageway. Then swiftly returned. They held their breath . . . but couldn't hear any rumble over their heads.

Gradually they all stepped out of the alcove, listening intently. Still nothing.

'It seems this deadly boulder isn't a problem. Shall we proceed?' enquired Master Tak. Reluctantly, they continued down the steep slope towards the vault. Suki was puzzled.

'Did Sensei Rika explain how the boulder resets itself?' she asked Bekko. 'What mechanism loads the trap again once it's been set off?'

'She said it's a magnetic rock. When

it reaches the other side of the curve, it latches again and charges up until it's triggered. OH!' Bekko suddenly realized why the boulder was taking so long to appear. It was coming from the other way! An ominous rumble ahead of them confirmed this theory that very instant.

'RUN!' screamed Suki. They all turned tail and bounded back up the passage, hotly pursued by a giant boulder that seemed intent on winning the race to the top. Tak sprinted ahead, reaching the alcove first. Suki and Bekko came perilously close to being squashed before arriving at the alcove, Suki pulling Bekko in behind her as the boulder thundered past. It briefly sucked the air out of the

passage before a rush of wind swept in . . . and the danger was gone. Lungs heaving, sweat dripping, feeling sick, they sat in darkness, shaking but feeling relieved to be alive. Suki was the first to recover, lighting a new torch and encouraging Bekko back on to his feet.

Master Tak seemed annoyed with himself for the lapse of focus and showing weakness in front of students. 'Are you all right, sir?' Suki asked, respectfully.

'Fine, fine! Let's get on!' he snapped. 'I'm assuming this rock is not going to make another attempt to murder us just yet?'

'N-n-no, sir,' Bekko said, gradually recovering his breathing. 'We're safe for now. It takes time to recharge.'

'Let's not waste any more time then.' Tak knew that Jirugi would be close behind them and needed to ensure Suki and Bekko had completed opening the vault before his master arrived to claim the medal. It would be embarrassing if his plan failed now! Soon they all stepped off the main passageway to light the lamp by the vault itself. Bekko found the switch easily, and the door rolled open. Suki lit the lamps inside.

'Does this door stay open on its own?' asked Tak.

'Yes, it does,' answered Suki, wondering why he wanted to know. 'We will close it when we leave. For now we just need to get comfortable and settle in until Sensei Rika gets here.'

'Aren't you going to show me the famous medal?' Tak enquired. 'Or any of these things?'

'Uh, sure, I mean, have a look.' Suki waved her arm to indicate all the treasures. 'We have plenty of time. Watch out for the jump across though.' She showed him the wide section where the ledge was hidden. 'This is the only safe place to cross.'

'Noted,' he said. Clearly fascinated and excited by all the magical objects piled up on the steps, he jumped over the chasm carefully and began to investigate. Bekko followed him. Suki was feeling very tired.

She sat down by the door. She knew it would be several hours before Sensei Rika would be there. She was worried about Kuma having to deal with Jirugi and Loko. And although she should feel glad that they had made it safely to the vault to keep watch over the medal, something definitely didn't feel right.

Bekko also couldn't shake the uneasy feeling. And strangely, being close to Master Tak didn't make him feel safer. Alarm bells were jangling in the back of his brain. Why? Was there something too . . . excited in Tak's face as he seized objects to examine? It didn't quite seem to fit with their mission to guard the vault patiently. Bekko didn't think Tak would have handled the objects like that if Sensei Rika was there.

'Sir? Shall we just wait with Suki? I don't think we should move anything. This is all dangerous stuff.'

Tak laughed grimly. 'Don't you worry, Bekko. Now, let's get a look at this Kokoro medal, shall we?' He leapt nimbly towards the glowing medal and whipped it off the statue, leaving Bekko open-mouthed.

Then a huge voice echoed his words. 'The Kokoro medal? Well done, Tak. I'll be taking that now. Hand it over.'

The gigantic shape of Jirugi invaded the doorway. Yunnan and Loko moved swiftly in behind him and grabbed Suki, who had

flown at Jirugi without a second thought.

Bekko's brain was doing backflips. Master Tak. A teacher! Some part of him needed to sit down and figure out how this could possibly be happening. He watched in utter disbelief as Tak descended the steps, leapt across the abyss, and knelt in front of Jirugi.

'Your loyal servant is proud to have captured this trophy from your enemies, Lord Jirugi.'

'Give me that!' Ignoring all ceremony, Jirugi snatched the medal from Tak, immediately placing it around his neck. 'How do I look?'

'Invincible, sir,' came the dutiful response from Tak, still kneeling. This clearly delighted Jirugi.

'Clever Tak! Thank you for your service. I never doubted you! So much better than that tanuki!' Jirugi's words annoyed Loko, but he and Yunnan had their hands full, tying a desperately wriggling Suki to the base of the lamp by the door.

'Let her go!' Bekko cried out, racing down the steps and leaping across the void to help his friend. However, Jirugi had other ideas. Seizing Bekko by the scruff of his neck, he held him in the air.

'What shall we do with these pesky cadets, Tak? This is the second time these two have tried to get in my way. I've had enough of it, frankly.'

'Personally, I'd drop the pair of them into the abyss,' shrugged Tak. 'Simple. But it might be worth seeing what else they know about the power of the medal. No one seems to know exactly how it works.'

'As if we would tell you anything, TRAITORS!' gasped Bekko.

'So brave, little warrior,' scoffed Jirugi. 'I think maybe your friend will tell me though. Especially if I hurt you!' He punched Bekko brutally, causing him to cry out in pain.

'Leave him alone!' Suki shouted.

'Don't tell them anything!' Bekko pleaded with her. 'They're going to kill us anyway. There's no point!'

'Shut up!' Jirugi slapped him furiously. Little did he know, there was a new warrior coming to Bekko's defence. One who particularly had reasons to detest the cruel mandrill. Crashing through the open door, Ishi snarled, snapped . . . and jumped, sinking his sharp teeth into Jirugi's leg. Jirugi howled and swung around, dropping Bekko. Bekko had no idea how the dog had managed to find him. He only knew that Ishi had saved his life. And had hurt Jirugi—despite the magic medal!

Ishi continued to attack Jirugi, viciously ripping at his arms and legs. Tak leapt on the dog from behind, using his stick to choke him unconscious. A momentary peace descended in the vault, broken only by Jirugi spitting on the ground. Bleeding and torn, he stood and ripped the medal from his neck.

'IT'S A LIE!' he bellowed. 'This medal is completely useless! It's about as protective as a banana. Actually, I think a banana would be more useful! This whole thing has been a total waste of time. Tak, you're fired! I don't want to see your ugly face back in my team. Loko, Yunnan, let's get out of here before those meddling guardians catch up with us.' In a towering rage, he stormed out of the room, Yunnan and Loko scurrying after him as fast as they could.

Tak looked mortified. 'Wait! Maybe there's something better here! Lord Jirugi! Wait!'

Bekko didn't know what to do. Free Suki? Tend to poor Ishi, who lay helpless on the ground? Both of these were important, but he was determined not to let Tak escape without a fight.

To get to the door, Tak had to get past Bekko. Realistically, Bekko knew that he was absolutely no match for the skills of the teacher, but he drew his stick. If he was going down, then he was going down swinging.

Master Tak couldn't resist teasing him as he saw the weapon appearing. 'Really, Bekko? You think I can't anticipate your every move? I taught you everything you know!'

'Not everything, sir,' Bekko glowered at him. 'You might have taught me some techniques, but I learned how to fight long before you showed up. I only wish I had been smart enough to see through you.'

'Don't be sorry. It's like I said. To know your enemy, you must BECOME your enemy. Jirugi will forgive me when he realizes how much I've learned about you all. The peaceful days of the Warrior Monkeys will soon be over.'

'Never,' Bekko replied, without hesitation. 'I have no fear of you. I will die if I must. You might beat me, but you will never beat us all. You can never win this fight! BANZAAAAAAAIIIIIII!' Bekko hurled himself at Tak.

Tak was caught by surprise. He suffered a few painful blows from Bekko before he began to fight back. His position was made more difficult because he was standing near the edge of the abyss, making it impossible to move safely. Bekko kept flying at him to strike. He was like a wasp, stinging and buzzing around his big opponent, never giving him a chance to find his balance. As Tak struck back, Bekko suddenly found that the constant blocking drills from training had become natural to him. He blessed Suki for making him train so hard. Her attacks in training had prepared him for what was really happening: someone was trying to knock him out, maybe even kill him.

Suki was not simply watching this fight unfold. She was chewing through the ropes as fast as she could. 'Hang on, Bekko! I'm coming to help you!'

And Bekko was hanging on. But Tak was so much stronger, and so skilful. Bekko couldn't dodge forever, and his own attacks were getting weaker as he lost his initial burst of crazy energy. First his fingers got whacked. Then, OUCH!,

Tak hit him with full force on the arm as he tried to defend himself. His arm hung, useless, and his stick fell to the ground.

Suki shook herself free then looked on in horror as Tak cornered Bekko, who was now on the very edge of the abyss. 'Time to see if this hole is deeper than your loyalty. Any last words? Suki, do you have anything to say to your friend before you follow him?'

'Yes! One thing. CATCH!' Seeing the Kokoro medal lying in the dirt, Suki grabbed it and flung it to Bekko, who instinctively put it over his head, just as Tak lunged forwards to push Bekko backwards to his death. The ruby in the medal glowed a deep red, and Bekko's

eyes widened as he seemed to surge with a powerful red shield. Instead of pushing Bekko off the edge, Tak's forceful attack took him straight through Bekko! Flailing and cursing, the evil traitor fell into the abyss. Suki, Bekko, and Ishi were alone again.

Their first thought was to check Ishi was breathing properly. Tenderly, Bekko rubbed the dog's back and gave him several firm pats to see if he could be woken up. It was such a relief to him to hear Ishi begin to cough. Ishi lifted his head, looking confused. Then he wagged his tail, seeing Bekko and Suki were safe in front of him, with no Jirugi threatening them any more. Gently, they encouraged him on to his feet.

'How did he find us?' Bekko wondered.

'I'm guessing he tracked your scent. That would explain how he made it over the quicksand. Clever boy. He saved us, Bekko, he saved us!' Suki was overwhelmed by what Ishi had done.

'And look, he's letting me pat him!' Bekko had tears in his eyes as Ishi leaned against him and put his head on Bekko's shoulder.

Suki blinked back tears too. It was time to be practical. 'Let me make a sling for your arm. It looks broken.' She used her stick to make a splint, and her belt for a sling. Then she looked up at the statue. 'Give me the medal, please, Bekko. I think we should put it back now.'

He took it off and handed it to her. She scrutinized it carefully. 'What does this mean, on the back?' She showed him the writing.

He examined the symbols. 'I don't know what some of these mean. This is "gift". This is "pure" and this is definitely "warrior". Look! The writing is disappearing!' The ruby was suddenly dull and faded, and the symbols on the back vanished.

'Did it work for you because I gave it to you?' Suki asked, curiously.

'Maybe it only worked because we were

trying to do the right thing. It certainly didn't work for Jirugi. Let's put it back anyway. We need to get back. I wonder what's happened to Kuma. Oh, crikey, Suki, do you think he is OK? Tak must have been lying about him being on patrol!'

Concern for their friend gave them fresh energy. Suki scampered up to replace the medal on Yotogi's statue. With Ishi leading the way, they went as quickly as they could back up to the surface. The sun was rising over the castle grounds as they ran to the gatehouse. The front gate was still propped open where Jirugi and his minions had made their escape. There was no sign of Kuma.

'KUMA! Where ARE you?'

'KUMA! Are you OK?'

A groaning noise caught their attention, and Ishi sniffed by the gate. He gave a series of little yaps. As Suki and Bekko went over to investigate, a very sorry-looking Kuma sat up looking dazed.

'Oh, my head!' he said. 'Where's Master Tak? He asked me to look out for Jirugi. I don't remember what happened next!'

'Kuma, oh Kuma, thank goodness you're OK!' Suki untied him and gave him a careful but huge hug.

'Have I missed something important, Suki-su?' he asked, rubbing the painful lump on his head.

'Something important . . . hmmmm . . .'
Suki frowned, wondering where to start.
'A few things, yes.' She counted them on
her fingers. 'Loko is a spy. Master Tak was a
traitor. Bekko's arm is broken. Master Tak
is dead. Jirugi was here. He's gone now. I
think that's probably most of it.'

Poor Kuma. It was too much to take
in. 'Did I really wake up? Or is this a
nightmare?'

Behind Suki, there was the sound of a
bear skidding to a halt.

'Good morning, Sensei Rika. Good
morning, Master Chan.' Bekko bowed as
Priya's passengers jumped down. Normally
very calm, they both looked distinctly

alarmed.

'What happened here? Is everyone all right?' Sensei Rika absorbed the scene: Suki, scruffier than ever without her belt. Bekko with a makeshift sling. Kuma looking battered and confused. Ishi guarding Bekko closely.

'Oh, Sensei.' Suddenly Suki was overwhelmed. 'I'm so sorry. We tried to protect the medal. We nearly lost it. We were tricked.'

Sensei Rika raised her eyebrows. 'Sounds like we have a bit of catching up to do.'

Much later, back in the Zen garden, Suki and Bekko sat watching Chan. Amid blossom fluttering in the breeze and the calming sounds of the rake on the gravel, they were trying to process what they had experienced together.

'What was the worst bit for you?' Suki asked Bekko. 'Was it fighting Tak? You were so brave! Your blocking was incredible!'

'I don't remember much about it,' confessed Bekko. 'The worst bit was when Jirugi put the medal on. I felt so scared! But then Ishi arrived to save us.'

Hearing his name, Ishi wagged his tail and looked up.

'What about you? What was the worst bit?' Bekko asked Suki.

'Definitely seeing you being attacked and not being able to help. That was awful! I feel like I was pretty useless in the battle,' said Suki, sadly.

'You mean apart from saving my life with the medal? That was quite helpful!' Bekko laughed, prodding Suki with his splint.

'Oh, yes. Apart from that. I suppose that did help a little bit,' smiled Suki. 'If I ever get to see those ancient guardians though, I'm going to have a few things to say. Quicksand, boulders, bottomless voids . . . the vault is a pretty deadly trap.'

'True,' Bekko agreed. 'Although in the end, it was only deadly for Master Tak.'

'"To know your enemy, you must become your enemy",' murmured Suki, thoughtfully. 'I don't ever want to be like Jirugi, but I think we are beginning to understand him a bit better now. He's the sort of person who cares more about himself than his friends. Does he even have any friends?'

'He doesn't have a friend like you, Suki, that's for sure. No one does.'

Flurries of thoughts and petals lifted and spiralled in the peaceful garden, sweeping the old gardener's hair. His meditation flowed into the swirling gravel patterns: the ever-changing path of the warrior.

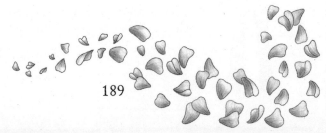

THE SPIRIT OF THE WARRIOR MONKEYS

BE ON TIME —To be early is to be on time. To be on time is to be late. To be late is . . . unforgiveable. Always treat others as you would like to be treated: never keep them waiting.

TRY YOUR BEST – If you're going to do something, really try your hardest. Always put in your best effort and energy. Growth is uncomfortable; accept it and do it anyway!

STAND TALL – Develop positive body language. Stand tall like a hero, and build trust with good eye contact.

LISTEN – Knowledge is power and your brain can never be full. Listen to advice. You don't always need to follow it but you can always learn more to help you make the best decisions.

DO A LITTLE EXTRA – Do you do enough? Or a bit more than enough? Making a little extra into a habit is a brilliant way to help yourself progress.

GET ORGANIZED – What do you need for the day? Look for what you need while you have time to look. You'll be prepared, and you'll be calm and ready to DO YOUR BEST!

Acknowledgements

The traps and puzzles in this book owe a great deal to the knowledge and ingenuity of others including my students John Allen and Billy Burnham (attempts to devise a non-magical way to roll and reset a boulder) and my friend James Long (patient suggestions of symbols which could be walked). Any errors are mine, not theirs, though.

I owe a special debt to the wonderful Monkey Haven on the Isle of Wight. This amazing place is a refuge for primates who have been bullied, illegally trafficked or unable to be integrated in other facilities. I'd especially like to mention Djimmy, who is the reason Bekko is a mangabey. Djimmy was found abandoned on a busy road in Germany and then kept in isolation for 7 years. The primate rescue charity AAP placed him with Monkey Haven and found him a friend (Buna) who was not accepted by her group in Barcelona zoo. They now live happily together. Djimmy is still very nervy and clings tightly to his security object – a toy pig which he loves dearly. You can read about the Monkey Haven at www. monkeyhaven.org or visit it near Newport IW.

M.C.STEVENS